Chris Higgins

Illustrated by **Lee Wildish**

Hodder
Children's
Books

A division of Hachette Children's Books

Hodder Children's Books
a division of Hachette Children's Books
338 Euston Road, London NW1 3BH
An Hachette UK company

For Vinny, Zac, Ella, Jake,
Bea and Louis

Chapter 1

On Saturday morning, we are all in the kitchen as normal, eating breakfast. My dad walks in with a sledgehammer, takes a swing, and knocks a big hole in the wall.

We all jump a mile.

Jellico, our crazy dog, barks wildly as clouds of dust rise into the air. We stare open-mouthed into next door's kitchen.

Uh-oh! **WORRY ALERT!**

'What did you do that for?' asks Mum.

'Because I wanted to,' says Dad, and grins at us all.

This is not normal behaviour for my dad. Or anyone else for that matter.

My brother Dontie's face lights up. 'Can I have a go?'

'No!' Mum and Dad say together and his face falls.

'You did!'

'I know,' says Dad, looking a bit sheepish. 'I couldn't resist it. But if you have a go everyone else will want one as well and the house will come crashing down around us.'

HUGE WORRY ALERT!

'It's not fair!' says my sister V, which is something she says a lot.

But I don't want a turn, and neither does my little brother Stanley, nor my little sister Anika, who has jumped off her seat and is clinging onto Stanley for safety. Our baby brother Will couldn't have a turn even if he wanted to because he's too little.

'What will Mr and Mrs Tidy say?' asks Stanley. We peer through the hole looking for angry neighbours but there's no sign of them.

Mr and Mrs Tidy get cross if our ball lands in their garden. They say it makes holes in their lawn. I think they will be very cross indeed now my dad has made a hole in their house.

'They won't say anything,' says Mum and I can't believe what she does next.

'Here,' she says with a gleam in her eye.

'Swapsies!' She dumps Will into Dad's arms and picks up the sledgehammer. 'Stand back kids,' she orders and swings it high over her head, bringing it crashing down against the wall.

The hole is bigger now. Bits of brick and cupboards land on Mr and Mrs Tidy's nice clean floor. What will they say?

HUMUNGOUS WORRY ALERT!

My parents have gone totally bonkers.

Chapter 2

Mum and Dad are rolling about on the floor, laughing hysterically.

'You should see your faces!' splutters Mum. Tears are pouring down her cheeks.

'It's sooooo funny,' says Dad, clutching his tummy.

We stare at them in disbelief. Someone's got to take charge in this family.

'No, it's not,' I stand over them with my hands on my hips like Mrs Dunnet, our headteacher. 'It's not funny for Mr and Mrs Tidy!'

My parents are acting worse than naughty boys in the playground. They are behaving like yobs (yob is 'boy' spelt backwards, by the way).

I have never seen them like this before.

V joins forces with me and puts her hands on her hips too. 'What do you think Grandma and Granddad would say if they saw you behaving like this?' she scolds. But Mum and Dad just shriek louder.

'We are very disappointed in both of you!' I say sternly and at last they come to their senses and get to their feet.

Mum scrubs at her face with a hanky. 'Sorry, Mattie!' she mumbles.

'Sorry everyone!' echoes Dad. But his

voice is high and squeaky like he's still trying not to laugh and Mum's shoulders start shaking again.

'Stop it this minute!' I warn them. 'You're upsetting the baby!'

This is not true. Will thinks it's funny. But it does the trick.

I am so proud of myself. I sound like a cross between Mrs Dunnet and Grandma. Mum and Dad take a deep breath and say sorry in their normal voices.

Then Dontie says, 'Oh, I get it!' and he starts laughing too. What is wrong with my family today?

'Get what?' asks V crossly. She hates to be left out.

'They've gone, haven't they?' grins Dontie. Dad nods.

'Who's gone?' asks Stanley, who, like V,

Anika and me, is struggling to keep up.

'Mr and Mrs Tidy. They moved out yesterday when you were at school.'

'So they don't live next door anymore?'

'No, they've moved away.'

'But ... that's still no reason to knock great big holes in their house.' V is really puzzled. I'm not surprised. When V tore up Stanley's prize book my parents were very cross with her. But now they're tearing down someone else's kitchen wall.

'Of course it isn't,' says Mum. 'But it's ours now. Remember? We said we were going to buy it and knock through, making both houses into one lovely big home for us all to live in. So it won't be a tight squeeze anymore.'

Oh, now I see! I knew that. I'd just forgotten about it when I saw my parents acting so crazily. Plus, now I come to think about it, I didn't really understand that knocking through actually meant … knocking through. With a sledgehammer.

'So … is that what we've got to do? Knock down the wall? And then we live in both bits.' I stare doubtfully through the hole in the wall at the rubble on next door's floor.

Anika's face falls. 'Don't like it!' she says, which is exactly what I'm thinking.

'Don't worry, darling,' says Mum – who is sensible again, thank goodness. She sweeps Anika up in her arms and gives her a big kiss. 'It will be lovely when it's finished, I promise you.'

Chapter 3

My mum is an optimist. An optimist is someone who always looks on the bright side and hopes for the best. She thinks our new knocked-through house is going to be lovely.

The opposite of an optimist is a pessimist.

I am a pessimist. A pessimist is someone who always expects the worst. I think our new knocked-through house could be a disaster.

Grandma says I've got an old head on young shoulders. This makes it sound as if I've got grey hair, wrinkles, false teeth and a nine-year-old's body, which is quite funny if you think about it.

I haven't, by the way.

She means: I'm a worrier. I don't like being a worrier but I can't help it. I was born that way.

Grandma, who has lots of sayings, also says that all the babies in our family arrived with their own personalities. She's right. I make a list of the personalities we were born with, in the order we were born. I like making lists.

1. Dontie: cocky
2. Me: worried
3. V: cross

4. Stanley: responsible
5. Anika: sunny
6. Will: smelly

I don't know what personality Dad was born with so I ask Mum.

'According to Grandma, he's perfect,' she says, so I add it to the list.

7. Dad: perfect

'What about you?' I ask. 'Were you born perfect, too?' and she makes a funny, snorty noise in her nose.

'Definitely not!'

Then I remember that actually, no one knows what Mum was like when she was born because she was brought up in care until she was fostered by Aunty

Etna and Uncle Vesuvius.

'What shall I put then?' I can feel worry coming on.

Mum does that gentle stroking thing with the side of her finger, down my cheek and around my chin, that makes my tummy go all soft and melty.

'Whatever you think, Mattie, love.'

So this is what I write down.

8. Mum: pretty and fun and kind and loving

Though personally I think she's perfect as well.

Anyway, because I'm a pessimist, I was worried when Dad picked up that sledgehammer and started knocking through into next door to make a bigger house for us all.

This is because, although my dad's a brilliant sculptor, when he does DIY things have a habit of going wrong.

DIY means Do It Yourself.

Here are some of the things my dad has DIYed that have gone wrong.

1. He fixed the broken tiles on the roof but put the ladder through the bedroom window.

2. He cleaned the chimney and got soot all over the house.

3. He put up shelves and they fell down Granddad's head.

4. He put a shower in over the bath and the shower head fell off and broke the bath in two.

5. He tried to fix the toaster and blew all the lights in the house.

6. He mended the crack in the toilet seat with extra strong glue and Uncle Vesuvius got stuck on it.

7. He drilled a hole in the wall to put a picture up and the drill went straight through a water pipe and flooded downstairs.

8. He put a fence up in our front garden and forgot to put a gate in it so we couldn't get out.

Maybe my dad's not so perfect after all.

Chapter 4

It turns out I needn't have worried after all. Because now we've got Bob and Jason.

'Bob the builder!' laughs Dontie, and Anika can't believe her luck. She thinks it's Bob the Builder off the telly, come to knock through into next door and make a big new house for her.

Jason is Bob's helper.

Bob is big and bald and red-faced and cheerful.

Jason is tall and curly-haired and brown-skinned and serious.

Bob is sort of in-between Granddad's age and Dad's.

Jason is sort of in-between Dad's age and Dontie's.

I like them both.

Bob is really funny. Mum says he should be in a pantomime. He asked Anika if she was married and she had a fit of the giggles, then he said he liked my hat and tried it on. He looked really silly with it perched on top of his big head.

(I don't mean he's a big-head like a show-off. I mean his head is very large, like the rest of him.)

Actually, he does show off, but in a nice way. He makes us laugh all the time. He tries to make Jason laugh too, but Jason just rolls his eyes and says he's heard it all before. Though sometimes, when Bob is being really silly, even he can't help smiling, and that makes Bob so happy he does a little dance which makes us laugh even more.

Anika and Will are lucky because they get to stay home every day with them. Will doesn't notice the banging and crashing, he sleeps through it mostly. But Anika trails after them all the time like a little dog. (Actually, our dog Jellico doesn't like the noise and stays in his basket with his paws over his ears.)

Bob had to warn Anika to keep away while they're working because it's dangerous, so she was sad. He bent down to speak to her, his hands on his knees.

'Tell you what, Annie, love, builders

need lots of tea. So when we have a break, can you make us a cuppa?'

Now, Mum says, Anika spends all day while we're at school collecting leaves in the garden for pretend cakes and biscuits. Then, when Bob and Jason are on a break, she serves them her 'treats' on her toy tea-set with pretend tea (which is actually water).

According to Anika, they eat and drink them all up.

'Yeah, right,' says V who's a bit sceptical (sceptical means you don't believe everything you hear). But I used to love playing with that tea-set when I was little and once I remember giving Dad grass on a plate and he said, 'Yummy! Spaghetti, my favourite!' and ate it all up.

By the way, Bob and Jason don't just sit around drinking pretend tea all day. They work really hard. Already they've knocked through downstairs and torn out Mr and Mrs Tidy's kitchen to make a nice big new one for us.

Tonight after Bob and Jason have left, Dad inspects what they've done so far.

'They're doing a good job aren't they?' says Mum.

'Not bad,' says Dad.

'Getting on nice and fast,' says Mum.

'Good,' says Dad. 'They'll be gone soon.'

'They're very professional,' says Mum.

'So they should be,' says Dad. 'We're paying them enough.'

I don't think my dad likes other people DIYing in his house.

I think my mum is a big fan of Bob and Jason.

'You know what the best thing of all is?' she asks with a cheeky grin.

'What?' answers Dad, grumpily.

'They haven't blown a fuse or burst a pipe or broken a window yet!'

Then she makes a quick dive for the stairs before Dad can catch her.

Chapter 5

My best friend in the whole world is Lucinda Packham-Wells. I didn't choose her, she chose me. She first sat next to me in reception and she's stayed sitting next to me ever since. She's very bossy but that's OK because I'm used to bossy people. My sister V is bossy and so is Grandma.

I like sitting next to Lucinda because she lets me use her sparkly pens. She always thinks she knows the answer so she's always got her hand up. Sometimes she gets it wrong but she doesn't mind. Lucinda is very confident and much braver than me.

That's why I was surprised that she cried when she heard we were moving away and I'd have to move schools. She was more upset than I was!

We were going to buy a posh new house in the country because we'd won the lottery (nobody knows this, it's a family secret in case people get jealous). But the house next door came up for sale and now we're knocking through instead.

I'm glad because I love school. We all do – even V, now she can read. None of us wanted to go to a different one.

I like my classroom and I like Lucinda and I like the rest of my class, even Alfie who picks his nose (though I wouldn't want to sit next to him), and I like my teacher, Mrs Shoutalot, (even though she shouts a lot).

Today it's cold and rainy outside but the classroom is warm and snug. Normally we would be doing literacy now but Mrs Shoutalot told us to get on with silent reading or silent drawing instead because she's very busy this morning.

She doesn't look very busy. She's sitting at her desk, gazing out of the window and sighing a lot. This is very unusual because normally she doesn't sit quietly, she flies around the classroom shouting and checking that you're OK, like a noisy guardian angel.

Another unusual thing is that she was late to class this morning. Mrs Shoutalot is a stickler for punctuality and often reminds us very loudly that 'I AM NEVER LATE AND I CANNOT ABIDE LATENESS IN OTHERS!' But today we were all there before her, wondering where she was.

I don't think it was her fault. The teachers were having a special meeting in the staffroom which had DO NOT DISTURB on the door in big letters and they probably wouldn't let her out.

They had a meeting last night as well. I know this because yesterday, when we were waiting for Mum after school, I saw Mr Kumar from the shop going in to see Mrs Dunnet and he's a governor. And other people I didn't know drew up in cars and went in clutching briefcases and files.

Mrs Shoutalot sees me watching her and I wait for her to shout, 'MATTIE BUTTERFIELD! GET ON WITH YOUR WORK!'

But something really strange happens. Instead of telling me off she looks guilty, picks up her pen and starts writing furiously, like I'm the teacher and she's the kid and I've caught her wasting time. Weird.

I go back to drawing Bob with my hat on.

Two minutes later I'm disturbed by a click-click-clicking noise. I look up and Mrs Shoutalot is tapping her pen against her teeth and staring out of the window again, in a world of her own.

The door opens. It's Miss Pocock, my teacher from last year. I **LOVE**

Miss Pocock. I smile at her and say, 'Hello, Miss!' but she ignores me and makes straight for Mrs Shoutalot, and arms folded, perches on the end of Mrs Shoutalot's desk. Then the two of them start whispering together and it goes on for ages and they don't even notice that no one is doing silent reading or drawing anymore.

'What's going on?' I ask Lucinda, who knows everything.

'Don't know. But we can find out.'

Chapter 6

It's turning into a really strange day. All the teachers are acting weirdly, not just ours.

They're in and out of each other's classrooms non-stop.

At one point we have four teachers in a huddle around Mrs Shoutalot's desk, taking no notice of us whatsoever, even though by now everyone has stopped pretending to read or draw and is chatting or messing about.

Then Mrs Shoutalot disappears for what seems like hours, which is really annoying because people get silly.

Someone makes a paper aeroplane and whizzes it around the room. Everyone joins in.

Lucinda, who gets giddy easily, snatches my picture of Bob and Jason and throws it out of the window.

Other people chuck things out of the window too. Rubbers and pencils, I mean, not desks and chairs.

We all swap places.

We sit on the tables.

Lewis does a squiggle on the whiteboard.

Holly runs out and sits in Mrs Shoutalot's chair for a dare and runs back again.

Mad Marcus climbs up onto Mrs Shoutalot's desk. Morgan pushes him off and he bangs his head and starts crying.

Lucinda offers to do a tap dance on top of Mrs Shoutalot's desk to make Mad Marcus better, if I keep watch at the door.

Luckily, everyone boos that idea, screws up their paper aeroplanes and chucks them at her instead.

After a while even the naughty boys are running out of ideas for messing about and we're all getting fed up. It's not much fun being naughty if there's no one to tell you off. People start going to the door and looking down the corridor to see if Miss Shoutalot is coming back.

At last Tia shouts, 'She's coming!' and everyone scurries back to their seats.

When Mrs Shoutalot comes in, we're all sitting down in our places like model pupils, silently reading and drawing.

'Good children!' she says, sitting down again at her desk, but she hardly looks at us. She doesn't seem to notice that her classroom isn't as tidy as usual, or that the tables and chairs have shifted places, or that her floor is littered with screwed-up paper aeroplanes, or that there's a squiggle on her whiteboard or that Mad Marcus has got a lump the size of an egg on his forehead. She just puts her chin back on her hand and carries on gazing out of that window, forgetting all about us.

At lunchtime the teachers have yet another meeting in the staffroom so we have an extra-long break. This sounds like fun but it's not because it's raining and we've been playing all morning. We're bored. They won't come out, not even in an emergency, which it is because Lucinda thinks she might have a splinter in her thumb. We have to knock six times before anyone answers.

'It's hard to tell,' Lucinda explains, when Miss Pocock appears at the staffroom door, hands on her hips. 'There's a lot of skin on the end of my thumb. But I think one might have gone in.'

'You'll live, Lucinda,' says Miss Pocock, who is normally very kind-hearted.

'Is there anything we can do to help?' asks Lucinda politely, craning her neck around Miss Pocock to peer into the staffroom behind her. 'We could wash up your coffee cups for you or ring the afternoon bell or answer the phone if you like?'

Miss Pocock points to the DO NOT DISTURB notice and puts her finger to her lips. Then she goes back inside and shuts the door.

Chapter 7

'Had a nice day?' asks Mum as I run out of school. She's standing just inside the gate waiting for us, with baby Will in the pram, Anika by her side and Jellico tied onto the handle.

Across the playground, the other mums are bunched up together, ignoring their kids and listening to Lucinda's mum holding forth. I can hear snatches of what she's saying.

'Friends at County Hall ... cuts to

the education budget ... not financially viable ... merge with another, maybe ... only a rumour, of course ...'

'What's Lucinda's mum going on about?' asks V as she makes her appearance with Stanley.

'Don't know,' says Mum, glancing over. 'I've only just got here. But there's one thing for sure. If she doesn't know about it ...'

'... it hasn't happened!' we all say together. Mrs Packham-Wells is famous for finding out things before anyone else.

'Come on,' says Mum. 'I need to stop off at Kumar's for something for tea. What d'you fancy?'

'Golden stars!' say Stanika. (In case you don't know this already, Stanika is Stanley and Anika together, which they always are, except when Stanley's at school.)

'Cheeburger and chips!' says V.

'Spag bog!' says me.

Actually, this is what we always say when we're asked what we want for

tea because these are our favourites. Dontie's is curry and rice, but Will doesn't count

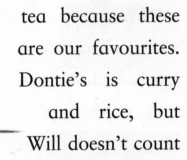

because he just drinks milk. It doesn't make any difference because Mum buys what she wants but it's nice to be asked.

Kumar's is very busy. In the end we get sausages, potatoes, onions and frozen peas for bangers and mash, crusty bread for mopping up, and yoghurts for afters. Yum! I can't wait.

At last it's our turn to pay. Mum puts her wire basket on the counter.

'How are you all?' asks Mr Kumar, who is always very polite. 'Did you work hard at school today?'

'Yes, Mr Kumar,' I say, to be polite back.

'No, we didn't!' says V, who never tells fibs. 'The teachers were too busy having talks to teach us.'

'Ah,' says Mr Kumar, looking wise. 'Maybe they had a lot to talk about.'

'Is there something going on up there?' asks Mum curiously.

Mr Kumar gives a little shrug. 'I'm afraid I'm not at liberty to say. If there is, you'll hear soon enough. It's a good school, yes?'

'Very good,' agrees Mum. 'Our Stanley was reading before he was five. He won the reading prize, you know. Our V had a few problems ...'

'Mu-um!' says V, embarrassed.

'... but they sorted them all out and now she's doing great, aren't you, love?'

V nods enthusiastically. 'I'm really good at maths.'

'Yes, she is,' says Mum. 'And Mattie loves it too, don't you?'

'Sometimes it's better than home,' I say. Mr Kumar and Mum laugh.

'Well, you couldn't pay a better compliment than that,' he says. 'Yes, it is a very good school.'

And then, just as we're going, he mumbles something so quietly I don't think Mum catches it, but I do.

'What a shame,' he says.

Chapter 8

Bob and Jason are in the Tidy part of the house. We can hear them banging away.

Dontie's not home yet. His school is further away than ours.

He says it's a rubbish school but Dad says he knows that's not true because he went there. I think Dad's right because Dontie didn't want to change schools when he had the chance. I think you have to say school's rubbish when you're at Big School.

Dad says Dontie's too cool for school now he's eleven going on twelve. Dontie says Dad's antique and you can tell because he uses the phrase 'too cool for school'.

I don't think he is, I think he's quite young for a dad. Lucinda's dad is antique, he's got grey hair and glasses like Granddad – but that might be because he's an accountant.

It's Dad's day off college where he teaches art. He's in the back garden with Uncle Vez looking at the shed.

Uncle Vez really is old, more Jurassic than antique. In fact he's a bit like a dinosaur because his skin is scaly from the sun and his face is all creased and cracked. A dinosaur in baggy trousers, braces and a battered old hat. I love Uncle Vez.

He's coming to live with us once the house is properly knocked through so that Mum can keep an eye on him. I can't wait! It's only fair because Uncle Vez and Aunty Etna were Mum's foster parents and they kept an eye on her when she was growing up. Now Aunty Etna is extinct.

I go into the back garden to check on my rabbit Hiccup in his hutch. The others follow me.

'You could have your own studio you know, Tim,' Uncle Vez is saying. 'You don't need to paint in this old shed anymore.'

'You just want it all for your garden tools!' laughs Dad. Then he looks around thoughtfully. 'You're right though. Now our garden's twice the size, I could build one out here.'

'Or we could have a swimming pool,' I suggest.

'Or a helicopter pad,' chips in V.

'And a helicopter ...' says Stanley hopefully.

'... 'elicopter,' echoes Anika.

'I'd settle for a nice conservatory,' says Mum.

We are so lucky. I used to worry all the time that we didn't have enough money to live on. Now we've got loads I don't have to worry anymore.

I bury my nose in Hiccup's warm, quivery fur. I don't really care whether we have a swimming pool or not. I've got everything I want. I'm just glad that I've grown out of being the family worry-worm at last. Mum said I would one day.

'What are you lot doing out here?' asks Dontie, appearing at the back door, munching an apple.

'Deciding between a helicopter pad and a swimming pool,' says Dad.

'Really?' says Dontie, then Dad laughs so he chucks the apple core at him. 'Stop winding me up. Have you heard the rumours?'

'What rumours?' says V.

'The school's closing down.'

'Yeah, right. Nice one,' snorts Dad. 'Sorry mate, you'll have to come up with a better excuse than that for avoiding your education.'

'I don't mean my school,' says Dontie, looking at V and Stanley and me. 'I mean theirs.'

I am so surprised I nearly drop Hiccup.

Forget everything I've just said about not being a worry-worm anymore.

MASSIVE, ENORMOUS WORRY ALERT!

Chapter 9

'I knew it! I knew something was up!' gasps Mum. 'That's what Camilla Packham-Wells was holding forth about in the school yard. If she doesn't know about it ...'

'... it hasn't happened,' finishes Dontie automatically.

Everyone stares at him open-mouthed.

'*Our* school?' says V, stunned.

'*My* school?' asks Stanley. Anika, who doesn't go to school yet but knows he's upset, slips her hand into his.

Dontie nods his head.

'How do you know?' asks Dad.

'Ryan Sharrat said. His mum's a teacher there.'

I remember Mrs Sharrat is Mrs Shoutalot's real name.

Mum can tell by my face that I'm really worried, and switches immediately into calming mode. 'He's probably got it wrong. Now don't you go fretting about it, Mattie.'

Dontie shrugs. 'He said that the teachers had a meeting last night with people from County Hall.'

I remember the grown-ups with briefcases filing into school.

'His mum's dead worried. It looks like she'll be out of a job,' continues Dontie.

I remember poor Mrs Shoutalot gazing out of the window and whispering with Miss Pocock.

'It's a good school,' says Dad. 'They won't close it down.'

I remember Mr Kumar saying the same thing: 'It is a good school.' But then he'd added, 'What a shame.'

'What will we do?' My voice sounds sort of strangled because I'm trying not to cry. 'Where will we go?'

'See what you've started now, Dontie?' says Mum crossly. 'You know what Mattie's like! She'll be awake all night worrying!'

'It's only a silly rumour,' says Dad.

'Just a bit of tittle-tattle,' soothes Uncle Vez.

'No truth in it whatsoever,' declares

Mum in her most matter-of-fact voice. 'Now scat you lot, so I can get tea on the go.'

Just gossip, that's all. Nothing to worry about. V, Stanley and me smile at each other in relief.

The doorbell rings and Mum rolls her eyes.

'Guess who?' she says wearily.

'Grandma and Granddad!' yells V, flinging open the door.

Grandma barges in. 'Have you heard the news? They're closing ...'

'... the school down! Yes, we've heard,' says Dad.

'It's all right Gran. It's just a silly rumour,' I explain to her.

'Playground gossip,' says Mum shortly. 'Camilla Packham-Wells getting everyone worked up, as usual.'

'It's not, you know!' says Grandma, whipping the evening newspaper out from beneath Granddad's armpit. 'It's all over the front page. Show them, Arnold!'

Chapter 10

It's in the evening newspaper in black and white. A big, bold headline:

CLOSURE OF LEARNWELL PRIMARY

followed by columns of print all about it.

There's even a picture of Mrs Dunnet, our headteacher, standing in front of the school, looking glum.

Mum and Dad pore over the article.

Dad keeps spitting out phrases like:

'Falling roles!'

'Under-subscribed!

'Reduce running costs!'

'Amalgamation process!'

'It doesn't make sense,' I say because I don't understand the big words.

'No, Mattie, it makes no sense whatsoever,' says Dad. 'Why haven't we been told about this?'

'I don't get it!' says Mum, looking bewildered. 'It's a great school. Why would they want to close it?'

My heart sinks into my toes. It's true then.

'Money!' says Granddad. 'It's always money.'

'It's the root of all evil,' says Uncle Vez and takes a puff of his biro.

'Where will we go to school now?' says V in a quiet little voice unlike her normal loud one. Poor V. She's only just settled down at school after a bad start. She won't want to begin all over again at a new one.

'It says here they're entering into a

federation with Teachem Hardway Primary,' reads Grandma. 'They're going to send them there instead.'

'Teachem Hardway!' shrieks Mum. 'That's miles away. How am I supposed to get them there every morning?'

'Teachem Hardway!' screeches V. 'That's where Lily Pickles used to go. She says the teachers tell you off if you get something wrong and the school dinners are horrible and make you sick!'

'Teachem Hardway!' Dontie pulls a face. 'We used to play them at football. They were rubbish and they were cheats. The only way they could get the ball was by tripping us up.'

'They used to be our arch-rivals when I was a kid,' frowned Dad. 'Over my dead body are my kids going to that school!

57

I'd rather home-school them myself.'

'Really?' says Mum, surprised.

'Really?' say all of us kids, just as surprised.

Actually I'm not quite sure what I think about staying at home and Dad teaching us. I mean, don't get me wrong, I like home but I like school as well. And as much as I love my dad, well I don't want him to be my teacher, do I?

Grandma: 'Don't be daft, you can't afford to give up your job.'

Me: 'What about Lucinda?'

V: 'What about Lily Pickles?'

Stanley: 'What about Rupert Rumble?'

Mum: 'You see? It's not just about lessons, is it, Tim? They need to be with their friends.'

Dad takes off the cap he wears all the

time and rubs his hand through his hair until it sticks up like a loo brush. Then he puts it back on again.

'Suppose so,' he says, then adds fiercely, 'but I tell you what. We're not giving in to this without a fight.'

'Now you're talking,' says Grandma.

Chapter 11

'I couldn't sleep last night for worrying,' I say to Lucinda the next day while we're waiting for Mrs Shoutalot to come to class. She's late again. 'I don't want to go to Teachem Hardway. They cheat at games and make you eat till you're sick and the teachers shout at you.'

'Mrs Shoutalot shouts at us,' she points out.

'That's different. That's because she's enthusiastic.'

'My mum says if the school closes she's not going to let me go to Teachem Hardway,' says Lucinda. 'She's going to send me to Davenports instead.'

'Miss Davenport's School for Young Ladies?' I say in surprise. 'The posh school in town with the boaters and blazers?'

Lucinda nods gloomily. 'Can you come with me?'

I think about it for a second. I wouldn't mind wearing a straw hat. 'Do you have to pay?'

'Loads. Dad says we can forget about holidays and Mum's got to cancel her gym subscription.'

'I won't be able to then,' I say automatically. 'We haven't got the money.'

Then I remember. Actually, we do have the money, now we've won the lottery. I keep forgetting all about it because Grandma said we're not allowed to tell anyone in case they get jealous.

'I don't want to go anyway,' says Lucinda and she sticks her chin out like she always does when she's made her mind up. 'I don't want to be a Young Lady, it's boring.'

I look around at Lewis and Morgan and Alfie and Mad Marcus and the other boys in our class doing daft things while they're waiting for our teacher, and think, well, at least it won't be boring at Teachem Hardway.

'Maybe you can persuade your mum to change her mind,' I suggest.

'You don't know my mum!' she says,

but I do. Then, to my horror, Lucinda's
eyes fill up with tears.

'I don't want to go!' she wails. 'I want
to stay here with you!'

Then I start crying too.

When Mrs Shoutalot walks in carrying
a big pile of letters and envelopes, she
doesn't tell us off. She just
hands us the big box of
tissues that sits on her

desk and tells us to wipe our eyes. Then she plucks a tissue out of the box for herself and blows her nose like a trumpet.

After that she chooses Lucinda and me to be her special helpers. We get to fold the letters up and stick them into the envelopes while the rest of the class has to do science. And at playtime she tells us to stay behind and lets us choose a chocolate from her special box.

I love Mrs Shoutalot. Then I remember that she won't be coming with us to Teachem Hardway and I feel really sad again.

At the end of the day we all get a letter to take home. We get three letters in our family but they all say the same thing.

They're full of more big words that

make my dad stamp and swear. I've never seen him so cross.

I think Bob and Jason are quite impressed.

Chapter 12

Our school hall is fit to bursting. It's like the church hall when we put the talent show on, people keep pouring through the door and there aren't enough chairs to go round. Mr McGibbon sends us off to fetch some more from the classrooms so we can cram everyone in.

It's funny to see the grown-ups perched on our titchy chairs. They flow over the edges, like icing on fairy cakes. With his legs crossed, Uncle Vez looks more like a garden gnome than ever. All he needs is a fishing line.

The letter said parents could bring their children with them if there were 'difficulties with child care'. Nearly all the kids are here, babies as well.

It didn't say you could bring grannies and granddads. Ours have come though and loads of others too. They probably went to the school themselves years ago, like Grandma. Alfie's even brought his great-grandma who's very old and deaf. She keeps asking when the bingo's going to start and Alfie's mum has to hush her up.

On the stage, Mrs Dunnet is sitting behind a table with a man and a lady. The man is in a suit and the lady is in a jacket and tight skirt and they look like the people from the lottery: all bright and smiley.

At last, Mrs Dunnet stands up and introduces them as Mr Costings and Miss Cutts from County Hall. She doesn't explain what County Hall is but I think it must be important.

Miss Cutts gets up first and makes a smiley speech about our school, praising it for its excellent work and recognizing its achievements and noting that it's succeeding against all the odds. This all sounds good to me. My dad starts clapping so I join in too.

But then he gets to his feet and says, 'Why do you want to close it then?' which I think is a bit rude to nice Miss Cutts and not like my dad at all. To my surprise, the audience starts clapping and cheering like he's said something clever, so I must've got it wrong.

Then Mr Costings stands up and talks about figures and projected numbers and surplus places and cost-effective management of resources and it all gets a bit boring.

The grown-ups in the audience must think so too because, do you know what they do? You're never going to believe this.

They start booing!

The kids in the audience sit up straight and stare at all the grown-ups who are booing and hissing at Mr Costings. If we did that to our teachers when they were boring, we'd be in **BIG TROUBLE!**

Grandma is a stickler for manners. Suddenly she shouts out, 'Shame on you!'

which is embarrassing but I don't blame her, the way people are behaving.

But then everyone else starts shouting, 'Shame!' too and I get it! Grandma, and everyone else, is shouting at Mr Costings!

Lucinda's dad (who's an accountant, so he should be used to being bored) yells, 'Pull the other one, it's got bells on!' and everyone laughs except for Mr Costings and Miss Cutts who are looking less bright and smiley by the minute.

I don't know what's got into the grown-ups in the audience. Even Mrs Dunnet, who is normally really strict in assembly, sits there with folded arms and an expression on her face like she's sucked a lemon by mistake, and doesn't do a thing about it.

Poor Mr Costings tries to keep going

but no one is listening to him, so after a while he gives up and sits down. Then Mrs Dunnet asks if anyone has any questions and a forest of hands shoots up.

I can't remember most of them but I feel proud of my grandma when she stands up and talks about 'strong, traditional values' and gets a round of applause.

I feel proud of my mum too because she asks Mr Costings, 'Why are you talking about falling numbers when the nursery is over-subscribed?' and everyone says 'Hear! Hear!' like they wish they'd thought of asking that question too.

The meeting goes on and on and on. After a while, Will and Anika fall asleep in Mum's and Dad's arms, Stan curls up on Granddad's lap, V slumps on her chair and I feel myself drifting off. Even

Mr Costings and Miss Cutts look as if they wish they were home in bed.

At last Mrs Dunnet says, 'I'll take one final question,' and she chooses Alfie's great-grandma who has had her hand up all night.

Alfie's great-grandma gets to her feet. 'What time does the bingo start?' she asks.

Then Mrs Dunnet declares the meeting closed and we all go home.

Chapter 13

Our old/new house is coming along nicely. The kitchen is twice the size it was and Bob and Jason have put in a new cooker, a new fridge-freezer and new blue cupboards. Today Bob's installing a dishwasher!

We're all excited about it except for Grandma.

'I'm not using that thing,' she says, eyeing it suspiciously as if it's about to explode. 'Hot water and elbow grease, that's all you need to wash up.'

'What's elbow grease?' asks Stanley and she says, 'A bit of effort,' which doesn't make sense because you need washing-up liquid and a sponge as well.

Actually, as I get older I'm learning a lot of things don't make sense. Like the proposed closure of our school.

It's Saturday morning and Mum and Dad have explained it all to us over breakfast. Grandma's come round to say her piece too.

Now I understand why all the parents were booing Mr Costings and Miss Cutts last night (though I still think it was a bit rude). And I also understand why my normally nice, kind dad was so angry.

You see, our family took a Democratic Decision not to move to the posh new house we were buying with our lottery win because we didn't want to move schools. We all had a vote, even baby Will (actually, Mum voted for him). OK, we didn't want to move away from Grandma, Granddad and Uncle Vez either, but that's not the point.

The point is, now our school is going to close, we're going to have to move schools after all. Not because it's a bad school, in fact it's a very good school, but because of Falling Numbers. This means there aren't enough kids in the area to keep it going.

'Well, we'll just have to have some more then to swell the numbers!' says Mum with a grin. Grandma looks alarmed and Bob drops his spanner with a loud clatter.

That's a good idea! I like babies, even

stinky ones like Will.

The doorbell rings. It's Lucinda and her mum.

'I hope you don't mind, but I thought we could have a chat about the meeting last night. Ooh!' says Lucinda's mum, looking around. 'You've been busy. Love the blue units.'

'Cup of tea?' asks Mum, looking amused. We all know that Lucinda's mum's been dying for an excuse to come round and have a look at our alterations.

'Closing the school is stupid!' announces Lucinda. 'There are loads of kids in our class, aren't there, Mattie? There's no room for anyone else.'

'There is in my class,' says V.

'And mine,' says Stanley.

Lucinda's mum sits herself down at the

table. 'But like you said at the meeting Mona, there are lots of children in the nursery and soon they'll be filtering through.'

'Yes, and we're going to have some more babies to help swell the numbers,' says V.

'Really?' squeaks Lucinda's mum, her nose twitching with curiosity.

'It's the middle of the school that's the problem,' says Dad gloomily. 'They won't pay teachers nowadays to stand in front of half-empty classes.'

'Yes, but it makes no sense,' says Mum. 'They've just had ten thousand pounds worth of play equipment from lottery funding. What a waste!'

'What do they want to close that lovely school down for?' says Grandma sorrowfully. 'I spent the best years of my life there.'

'Money,' says Bob, crawling out from behind the dishwasher. He sounds like Granddad and Uncle Vez. 'That's what their game is. It's a prime site for development that school building. They'll be wanting to sell it off for flats. I'd buy it if I could afford it.'

Grandma glares at him and he changes his mind quickly. 'I wouldn't really,' he says and stands up and pushes the dishwasher into place. 'All ready to use.'

But no one's interested in the dishwasher anymore.

'So there you go,' sighs Mum. 'They'll merge the two schools, make our teachers redundant and sell off the building. And there's not a damn thing anyone can do about it.'

'Oh yes there is!' says Grandma on her high horse. 'That school is closing down over my dead body!'

'In that case,' says Lucinda's mum, taking a flowery notebook and matching pen from her handbag, 'we need to organize a proper campaign.'

Chapter 14

It doesn't take long to organise a campaign when you're Lucinda's mum.

'Let's form a committee,' she says. 'I'll be chairman. Now, let me see, we'll need a few more people.' She rummages in her bag for her smartphone. 'Jonathan Wackham is a useful person to have on your side at a time like this.'

In no time at all, summoned by Lucinda's mum, the newly-formed committee is sitting around our kitchen table. Us kids are allowed to stay and listen as long as we're quiet.

The committee consists of:

Lucinda's mum
Lucinda's dad
My mum
My dad
Grandma
Mr Kumar (who's resigned from the school governors in protest)
Jonathan Wackham (who turns out to be Naughty George's dad and is on the council)
Rupert Rumble's mum

'I would like to propose Mrs Butterfield Senior as secretary,' says Lucinda's mum.

She means Grandma, not Mum.

'Seconded,' says Mr Kumar.

'Could you take the minutes, Mrs Butterfield?' asks Lucinda's mum.

'Delighted,' says Grandma, looking pink and pleased. 'Mattie? A pen and paper please.' I grab the ones by the phone and hand them to her.

'Meeting is called to order,' says Lucinda's mum. 'Item one: Proposed action to prevent the closure of Learnwell Primary.'

'What we need are ideas to co-ordinate a carefully-constructed grassroots campaign,' says Jonathan Wackham who knows lots of big words because he's on the council.

The ideas come thick and fast.

'I propose we start a petition!' says Grandma, writing it down.

Mr Kumar: 'I would like to organize a protest march.'

Jonathan Wackham: 'Excellent! Then we can take the petition to County Hall and demonstrate outside!'

Dad: 'We should let the Gazette know.'

Mum: 'And local radio.'

Jonathan Wackham: 'I'll get in touch with our MP.'

Lucinda's mum: 'I've got his number here. I go to pilates with his wife, you know.'

Grandma (scribbling like mad): 'How do you spell pilates?'

Rupert Rumble's mum: 'I think we should set up a Facebook page.'

Mr Kumar: 'Marvellous idea. We could call it *Save Our School*.'

Rupert Rumble's mum: 'I'll do that!'

Lucinda's mum: 'And I'll get it out on Twitter.'

Rupert Rumble's mum: 'It's all about social networking, you know.'

The committee members beam at each other, very pleased with themselves.

'In that case,' suggests Dontie. 'You should make a video and put it on YouTube.'

All the committee members look at him in surprise.

'What sort of video?' asks Dad.

Dontie shrugs. 'I dunno. A rap? Dancing? Something entertaining that will appeal to lots of people.'

Dad grins. 'Yeah, I like it. Get the message out to the bros.'

Dontie rolls his eyes.

'I think it's a great idea,' says Mum. 'But you should organize it, Dontie, not your dad.'

'Ok,' says Dontie. 'But you've all got to be in it.'

Chapter 15

Within days we're famous. Our Facebook page, Save Our School, has already had over 2,000 likes and people are talking about us on Twitter. And we haven't even done our video yet!

Most of it is down to Grandma. Now she's secretary of the Save Our School campaign, she's bought herself a smartphone like Lucinda's mum's and she tweets all day long. She's already got 1,251 followers.

Ping! Whistle! Grandma swipes her phone. 1,252.

'I'm sick of the sound of that thing going off,' grumbles Granddad. 'Do you know, she hasn't cooked a meal since all this started. We're living on beans on toast.'

'You'll survive,' says Grandma poking him in his round belly. 'Anyway, you can cook! I didn't burn my bra back in the Sixties to be at your beck and call, Arnold Butterfield. I've got a school to save!'

I think Grandma's loving this. I haven't seen her so full of beans since we did the talent show.

Literally.

Weirdly, although our school is now officially threatened with closure, everyone seems much happier, including the teachers. It's like they know we're on their side and we're all pulling together. It feels a bit like Christmas because we're doing fun activities like arts and crafts, only really it's banner-making for our march.

Granddad and Uncle Vez come in to help us. We spend all day long making placards and banners out of bits of wood and cardboard and potato sacks and old sheets and cereal packets and anything else we can lay our hands on. Then my dad helps us paint pictures and write slogans on them, because he's an artist.

Mine and Lucinda's says:

HANDS OFF OUR SCHOOL!

'We're certainly ticking our literacy boxes,' says Mrs Shoutalot cheerfully to

Mrs Dunnet and corrects Alfie's banner which reads, **LEAF ARE SKOOL ALOAN!**

Our headteacher has come into our classroom to see how we're getting on. 'And our art and design requirements,' she remarks. 'Love the skull and crossbones effect, Lewis.'

Then she whispers to Mrs Shoutalot, 'Just about sums it all up, don't you think? I feel like pirates are trying to steal our ship and make me walk the plank.'

'Don't worry, Miss, we'll save you,' I say. 'The Save Our School campaigners are making a video tonight at our house. It's going on YouTube.'

'YouTube!' says Mrs Dunnet faintly.

That's funny: me, Mattie Worry-Worm, telling my headteacher not to worry. But

I've got a good feeling about all this now we're actually doing something about it.

I am so excited about the video. Grandma wanted to film it for us on her new smartphone but Mum says she's got to be in it too, so Jason's going to do it instead.

I can't wait.

Chapter 16

We have tea early so we can clear away before everyone comes.

Mum makes us all help because she says if her new kitchen is going to be plastered all over the internet then it's got to be spotless. I think she's turning into Grandma (the old Grandma, not the new one). She even puts the kettle away in the cupboard!

'It's not fair!' grumbles V, but she does as she's told and loads the dishwasher.

I'm in charge of Will while Mum scours the cooker and Dad and Dontie move the table and chairs out of the way. Then Stanika sweep the floor with the dustpan and brush and Dad mops it over.

'I'm the director. I shouldn't have to do anything,' complains Dontie.

'You're not Quentin Flipping Tarantino, you know!' says Mum and makes him take the rubbish out. Poor old Jellico has to stay in his basket so he doesn't get dog hairs over our nice clean floor. He lays his head on his paws and winks at us sadly.

'How do?' says Uncle Vez, wandering in. 'Goodness me! Am I in the wrong house?'

'Ha ha!' says Mum. 'Don't sit down.'

'Why not? I've come for me tea,' says

Uncle Vez, surprised.

'Too late, we've tidied up. You'll have to wait till after the video.'

Uncle Vez mutters something that sounds like, 'bossy blooming women', under his breath. Jellico whines in agreement and both of them slope away outside.

'Don't disappear!' yells Mum. 'You're in it!'

At last we're all ready to go.

Lucinda and her mum and dad are the first to arrive.

Lucinda's mum's had her hair and nails done and is wearing a posh new outfit. Mum takes one look at her and says, 'I'll go and get changed.'

Grandma and Granddad arrive next.

OMG! We all stare at Grandma in surprise.

Grandma's had her hair done too. It's green with a red and white quiff at the front! Poor Grandma.

'Did it go wrong?' asks V.

'No, no, it's school colours,' explains Grandma cheerfully. 'Got to show support.'

'Rupert Rumble's here!' shouts Stanley. 'And his mum.'

'Naughty George is here too!' cries V. 'And his dad.'

'So it's just Mr Kumar we're waiting for,' says Mum, clattering downstairs in her best top, skinny jeans, dangly earrings and a cloud of perfume. 'Ooh, Marjorie! Loving the hair. Is it wash-in/wash-out?'

'Hope so,' says Granddad gloomily.

'You smell gorgeous, Mum,' says V.

'Shame you won't be able to smell

it on the video,' says Dad.

'You will on Grandma's phone,' says Dontie, winking at him. 'It's brand-new, state of the art. See, Grandma, this is the smell app.'

Grandma, who's not wearing her glasses, peers blindly at the screen.

When Jason appears he doesn't bat an eyelid at her green hair or when she tells him she can record smells on her phone. I think he's getting used to the Butterfields.

Time goes on and still Mr Kumar hasn't arrived.

'Where's he got to?' says Grandma, who can't wait to get started.

Jason looks at his watch. 'Better get a move on. I've got football training at 7.'

'Mattie? Pop along and fetch him,' says Mum.

'Fetch who?' asks Uncle Vez, coming back in with Jellico.

'Mr Kumar from the shop.'

'He's not there,' says Uncle Vez. 'I saw him going off in his car half an hour ago.'

'He must've forgotten,' says Dontie, cross. 'Shall we start without him?'

'I don't know,' says Jonathan Wackham. 'It would be good to have him on the video, what with him being an ex-governor.'

'He's here!' shouts Stanley who's been watching out for him.

'Oh no!' cries V. 'Look who he's got with him!'

We all rush to the window.

Mrs Dunnet, Mrs Shoutalot, Miss Pocock and Mr McGibbon are getting out of his car.

My heart sinks. It's all my fault for telling Mrs Dunnet.

Grandma folds her arms. 'If they think they're going to stop us making this video, they've got another thing coming!'

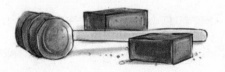

Chapter 17

Guess what?

Our teachers haven't come to stop us. They've come to join us! They want to be in the video too.

Dontie frowns. 'I need to think about this,' he says and goes off to confer with Lucinda's mum who's already planned a dance routine.

The teachers wait anxiously.

'Hurry up, mate!' shouts Jason. 'I've got football training at 7.'

Dontie comes back. 'Ok, we can fit you in. But you've got to do as you're told,' he says sternly.

'We will,' says Mrs Dunnet.

'Thank you,' says Miss Pocock.

'We've had to rethink what we were planning to do now there are more people,' he explains.

'Sorry,' says Mrs Shoutalot.

'No worries,' he says. 'It's just a few cheesy moves that will be easy to copy. We're thinking bouncing up and down to the music, pretending that you're riding a horse, shuffling sideways, and twirling your arms in the air like you're lassoing something.'

'Wicked!' says Mr McGibbon and waves his long arms about to give it a try.

'Hmm,' says Dontie, dubiously. 'Look,

just follow Lucinda and her mum and you can't go wrong. Now listen …'

He and Lucinda's mum and the teachers get in a huddle. All we can hear is squeaks and shrieks and giggles.

'Do you think they've got starring roles?' asks V, suspiciously.

'Looks like,' says Mum.

'That's not fair!'

'Dontie knows what he's doing,' says Dad.

'That's a first!' says Mum.

'I've got football training in half an hour!' shouts Jason and the huddle breaks up.

'Right, let's get on with it,' says Dontie. So we do.

Dontie plays us a really catchy beat on his iPod.

Lucinda's mum and Lucinda demonstrate the moves to go with it.

We all copy them.

Simple!

Some people are really good at it.

People like Lucinda and Lucinda's mum (obviously), Dontie, Miss Pocock, Naughty George, Mum, and Will who laughs his head off in Mum's arms all the way through.

Some people are quite good and can keep up.

People like me (I'm not boasting, it's true), Stanley, V, Dad, Rupert Rumble's mum, Mr Kumar, Mrs Dunnet, Naughty George's dad and Mrs Shoutalot.

Some people can't keep up at all and do their own thing.

People like Granddad who march,

Anika who shakes her bottom, Grandma who shakes her bottom and everything else as well, Mr McGibbon who waves his arms about like Mr Tickle, and Uncle Vez who does the twist with Bob the builder who asks if he can join in too.

When we've practised the moves and Dontie has put us all in position (Uncle Vez and Bob the builder at the back), he teaches us the lyrics. Now I know why the teachers were giggling. It's a sort of rap and really easy to learn. We run through it till we're word perfect.

'I've got football training in ten minutes,' Jason reminds us.

'Right, let's go!' says Dontie and suddenly I've got butterflies in my tummy, just like I did before our talent show.

'Don't worry,' says Jason, 'it's only a practice. Just enjoy it.'

The music begins and we start bouncing, trotting, shuffling and twirling to the beat. Before long we're sort of all doing it together.

'Now!' says Dontie, and Mrs Dunnet leaves her position, skips right up to the camera and says in a tough-guy voice,

'Don't close our school,'

and the rest of us answer in tough-guy voices,

'Cos that ain't cool.'

Next Mrs Shoutalot marches up to the camera and shouts,

'Don't need no federation,'

and we all shout back,

'Cos *we're one nation!*'

Then Miss Pocock shimmies up to the camera and asks,

'*Wanna get on a bus?*'

and we all yell,

'*Nah! Just wanna be us!*'

Mr McGibbon wags his finger sternly at the camera and says,

'*Hands off our school,*'

and we all wag our fingers at the camera too and say,

'*That's the rule.*'

We keep on repeating it and repeating it.

Uh oh! Dontie's forgotten to work out how to end it. Then Grandma comes to the rescue.

All of a sudden she shimmies her way to the front, flings her arms in the air and does the splits!

We're so surprised we burst out laughing as Dad and Granddad haul her up off the floor.

'Oh my word, I've done myself a mischief!' she says. 'I didn't know I could still do that!'

We play it back and it's really funny.

'Right then, let's do the real thing,' says Dontie.

'Sorry, can't do,' says Jason, 'I've got football training in two minutes,' and he uploads it straight to YouTube.

By the next morning it's gone viral.

Chapter 18

Today is the day of our protest march.
We are walking from school to County
Hall. It's a long way.

We assemble in the playground in
our form groups with our banners and
placards. Mums and dads and pre-
school kids line up behind us and lots of
other people have come to join in too.
The queue snakes right out of the school
gates and back down the main road of
our village.

Dontie says our Facebook page has had over 10,000 likes, our YouTube video has had 40,000 hits and we're trending on Twitter. He's mad he's missing the march because he's in Big School.

A man is going round interviewing people with a big furry microphone and another man is filming it with a big camera on wheels. It's BBC Television. When Mum speaks to him, baby Will tries to take a bite out of the microphone and everyone laughs. A lady from the local paper takes a photo of him.

'We're going to be on the telly!' Lucinda can't stop jiggling about with excitement.

A police car arrives to escort us and we set off behind our school band, who are playing something loud and rousing on their trumpets and drums. Mrs Dunnet leads the way holding a 'Save Our School' placard, followed by the nursery who are waving balloons and flags and the main school classes who are carrying more placards and banners. Everyone else, including the rest of my funny family, brings up the rear.

'This is going to be fun!' squeals Lucinda. 'Look how long our march is!'

It takes a long time to walk into town along the narrow, winding country lanes. After a while the littlies in the nursery get tired and want to be picked up. The lady from the local paper takes photos of their mums and dads having to carry them.

Tractors and cars keep having to pull into the side to let us pass. Lucinda and

I wave to them. Some drivers wave back but some look cross. The newspaper lady snaps photos of them too.

At last we get to town. People come to a stop when they see us coming, and cheer and clap.

'I feel like a celebrity,' says Lucinda, skipping with happiness. 'I wish we could do this every day!'

We march past Teachem Hardway Primary, the school they want to federate us with. It's big, dark and forbidding and looks like it's frowning at us and I don't want to go there. On we go to County Hall where our MP, Mr Fareham, is waiting for us on the steps.

MP stands for Member of Parliament which means someone who makes the laws of our land. Mr Fareham knows we don't want our school to close down because his wife does pilates with Lucinda's mum so he's going to show our petition to the Prime Minister. This is known as the Democratic Process.

Our Stanley has been chosen to hand over the

petition to him.

Mrs Dunnet says she chose Stanley because he's dependable. Lucinda says Mrs Dunnet chose him because he's cute. Either way, Mum and Grandma are bursting with pride, especially when the MP who's very tall bends down to shake hands with Stanley who's very small, and cameras flash on and off like Christmas tree lights.

Then we walk all the way back to school.

It's not exciting anymore and it seems much further now it's started raining. Soon we're freezing cold and wet through. We trudge along, soaked to the skin, and the lady from the paper runs up and down, snapping away at us with her camera.

'I'm tired out,' complains Lucinda,

dragging her feet. 'I'm glad we don't have to do this every day.'

I bite my lip. If our school closes down, Lucinda's dad will drive her to Miss Davenport's School for Young Ladies in his nice warm car.

But some people will have to walk this far every single day, whatever the weather.

Chapter 19

When we get back to school, Mrs Dunnet lets us go home early with our mums and dads because we're soaked through.

At home we strip off our wet clothes and rub our hair dry and get into the onesies Grandma bought us at the market. Bob and Jason have been busy, they've knocked through the two sitting rooms to make one big lounge.

We cuddle up together on the sofa and Dad makes us hot chocolate and hot buttered toast to warm us up. Then we spend the rest of the afternoon reading, playing board games, watching TV and grabbing baby Will every time he tries to dive off the sofa. It feels like Christmas.

Mum smiles at Dad. 'Funny, isn't it? It was always such a tight squeeze but now we've got all this space and here we are, still crammed together on the sofa.'

'Alright for some,' says Dontie moodily. He's just come in from school wet through to find us all hanging out together, warm and snug.

'Room for you too,' says Mum, hauling baby Will onto her lap and patting the space beside her.

'No thanks, got work to do,' says Dontie and slopes off to his room to play games on his new computer.

'Nearly time for the news,' says Dad, flicking over the channel. 'Wonder if the march will be on it?'

'Are we going to be on the telly?' asks V in excitement.

'Not the national news, but we may be on the local,' says Mum.

The national news is on first and is very boring, so I get back to my book which is far more interesting. After a while Dontie comes clattering down the stairs.

'Come and see this! The campaign's gone mental!'

We crowd into Dontie's bedroom and stare at his computer.

Our Facebook page has had 25,000 likes.

'Look at all these messages!' gasps Mum, reading them aloud. *'Our school is facing closure like yours ... Our school closed down last year ... We amalgamated with two other schools ... My children have to travel six miles to their new school. This is happening all over the country!'*

'And we're trending on Twitter,' says Dontie and clicks on to it so we can see similar messages of concern and support.

'Webpage, you won't believe ...' He opens up a stream of emails.

'And, wait till you see this ...' He clicks onto YouTube. 'It's gone crazy!'

'Flip!' says Dad, looking at all the hits our video has received.

'Local news!' shouts Mum and we dash downstairs just in time to catch Will trying to take a bite of the microphone.

'Are we famous?' asks Stanley.

'Do you know, I think we might be,' says Dad, grinning from ear to ear.

'One thing's for sure,' says Mum, her eyes shining. 'All this publicity is brilliant. They won't dare to close the school after this.'

Chapter 20

For a while it looks like my mum is right.

She and Grandma and Lucinda's mum set up Campaign Headquarters in our kitchen. They're mega-busy all day long, replying to the thousands of emails, tweets and messages that come flooding in, while Will sleeps soundly beside them. Mum has treated Grandma and herself to a new laptop each (Lucinda's mum's already got her own).

The local weekly paper prints a double-page spread of the march under the headline 'Save Our School'.

'Nice picture of you and baby Will, Mona,' says Grandma. 'Ooh! There's one of our Stanley shaking hands with the MP.'

Mum shines with pride. Then her face changes, 'Oh, look at those poor little mites soaked through.'

'Ah, bless!' says Grandma. 'Still, it's worth it if it means they won't have to do that trek every day, just to go to school.'

'Mrs Dunnet says she's had quite a lot of donations from the general public,' says Lucinda's mum.

'It's all looking really hopeful,' says Mum with satisfaction.

But she's wrong.

Before long the emails, tweets and messages start to dry up.

Tonight, on her laptop, Mum's looking puzzled. 'I can't understand it? I've only had three messages on Facebook today and two emails.'

'Yesterday's news,' says Dontie gloomily. He's been checking YouTube and discovered that a video uploaded this morning with a baby sucking a lemon has had loads more hits than ours.

'Listen!' says Dad and turns up the volume on the telly. A spokesman from County Hall is talking about our school using big words, some of which I've heard before.

'Despite public opinion ... the situation is unfortunately irredeemable ... falling roles ... insufficient funding available to pay the teachers' salaries for the next two years ... no alternative but to close the school ...'

We all gasp.

'What? After all we've done!' says Mum, looking shocked.

Dad gives a big sigh. 'It looks like we

may have come to the end of the road, love.'

'No way! Those teachers won't care, they'll do it for nothing!' says Mum defiantly.

'No they won't,' says Dad flatly. 'They've got mortgages to pay and mouths to feed, same as everyone else.'

'Didn't you say that the school's had lots of donations?' says Dontie. 'They could use those to pay the teachers' wages.'

'Brilliant!' says Mum and leaps up to phone Mrs Dunnet. But when she's finished talking she doesn't look happy.

'How much?' asks Dad.

'£378.63p,' says Mum.

'That's loads!' I shout in delight but Mum shakes her head.

'It's not enough, Mattie love.' She gives us a sad smile. 'It looks like the school is going to have to close after all.'

That's when I start to cry.

Chapter 21

I'm not the only one who cries when we hear that the school is closing in spite of all our hard work to save it. V and Stanley and Anika burst into tears as well, though actually I think Anika is only crying because Stanley is.

We stand in a line and howl. Tears spill from Mum's eyes and Dad and Dontie look really sad and that makes us howl even louder. Jellico joins in too. Only baby Will giggles because he thinks we're playing but we're not.

'It's not fair!' bawls V and Dad says, 'No, you're right V, it's not fair at all.'

'It's all my fault!' I wail.

'No it's not, Mattie!' says Mum. 'It's nothing you've done.'

'No. It's what I haven't done. I should've worried more. I should've made a Worry List!'

'It wouldn't have made any difference,' says Mum.

'Yes it would! You told me. You said, write your worries down and they won't come true. But I forgot! I was too busy with the campaign!' I burst into fresh wails.

'You said you'd save our school,' V glowers at Mum and Dad, her face wet and cross. 'That's what the campaign was all about.'

'I'm sorry, V,' says Dad, and now he looks as if he's going to cry too. 'I thought we could.'

'You said if I gave the petition to the MP it wouldn't close down,' sobs Stanley. 'Did I do it wrong?'

'No!' says Mum, dumping Will into Dad's arms and sweeping Stanley up instead. 'You did it beautifully, you brave little soldier! You're all soldiers! There's never been a better-fought campaign!'

'So why did we lose it then?' says Dontie flatly. Poor Dontie. He'd tried so hard to help us with that video and he doesn't even go to our school anymore.

'Money,' says Mum sadly. 'Mrs Dunnet says it will cost about £250,000 to pay the teachers' salaries until student numbers are back up again.'

'Two hundred and fifty thousand pounds!' I stare at Mum open-mouthed.

'That's a quarter of a million,' says V who's good at maths. 'I didn't know teachers were paid that much!'

Suddenly, the solution hits me. 'Let's ask for more donations then. Loads and loads. Until we get enough to pay their wages.'

'It would take too long,' says Mum. 'Anyway, people haven't got that sort of money. Not around here.'

'Dontie could put it on the internet.'

'I already have,' says Dontie. 'Website, Facebook, Twitter, YouTube, you name it. It's too late. People have moved on to something else.'

'It's over, Mattie,' says Dad firmly and I start crying again.

This is the **WORST** day of my life.

Chapter 22

The next day breakfast is horrible. Everyone's miserable, even Jellico, and nobody feels like talking. Only baby Will is normal, making happy grunting noises to get our attention, but when we don't make them back to him he falls asleep.

It's me who finally breaks the silence.

'When will the school close, Dad?' I've been worrying about it all night long. I want him to say it won't, it's all a mistake, but instead he sighs heavily.

'We don't know, Mattie.'

'We can find out,' adds Mum hastily but it's too late. Two big fat tears have spilled from my eyes, rolled down my cheeks and dropped off my chin into my cornflakes. V starts sobbing. I don't cry out loud because I know my mum and dad are just as unhappy as we are.

We walk to school in silence because there's nothing left to say. Lots of parents are milling around in the playground but inside, school is as hushed as a hospital. The teachers are hurt and no one wants to make them suffer any more, not even the naughty boys.

All morning parents queue up to see Mrs Dunnet.

'Look, there's your mum and dad!' says Lucinda as we're coming back

from lunch. I catch sight of them disappearing into her office.

'They've come to find out when the school is going to close,' I say, a lump in my throat.

'My mum's already enrolled me in Miss Davenport's,' she says, then her chin juts out and she adds fiercely, 'I'm not going!'

But we both know she'll have to.

In the afternoon, Mrs Shoutalot is reading us a story when there's a knock on our door.

'Come in,' says our teacher, even though you can't see anyone through the glass. The door opens and my brother Stanley is standing there. Stan is often sent to deliver important messages around the school because he's very reliable.

'Special Assembly, Miss,' he says,

importantly. 'Five minutes.'

We all line up and walk into the hall and sit down cross-legged. Mrs Dunnet walks onto the stage and my heart tightens with fear.

She's going to tell us when the school is closing.

Please don't let it be today.

Chapter 23

Yesterday was the **WORST** day of my life.

Today is the **BEST**!

I can't wait to tell Mum. The bell goes and I run outside waving my letter. Everyone else in the school runs outside waving their letters too.

Mum is waiting for us with Will in the pram and Jellico on the lead. And, surprisingly, Dad is here too with Anika on his shoulders!

'Mum! Dad! We've just had a special

assembly and Mrs Dunnet gave out these letters for the parents. Read this!' I thrust the letter at them just as V and Stanley thrust theirs at them too.

'Which one first?' laughs Dad.

'Mine!' says V.

'Mine!' says Stanley.

'It doesn't matter, they're all the same,' I say. 'Just read it!'

'Tell you what V, you read it to us,' says Dad.

V tears open the envelope, shakes out the single sheet of paper and puts on her important reading voice.

'Dear Parents,

On behalf of the headteacher and the governors of Learnwell School I am delighted to inform you that, thanks to

the generosity of one amom ... amon ...
anom ...'

'... anonymous,' I insert helpfully,

'... anonymous benefactor who has
donated a sum of money sufficient to pay
the teachers' salaries for the next two
years, the school will no longer amal ...
amalg ...

'... amalgamate,' suggests Stanley
who's a brilliant reader for his age,

'... amalgamate with Teachem
Hardway but will remain open and
continue to serve the children of our
community in its own unique and profic
... profish ... procish ...'

'... proficient,' says Dad, with a big
grin on his face,

'... proficient way.
Yours faithfully ...'

V doesn't get to finish because Dad whoops with delight and sweeps us all up into a big funny family bear-hug. Jellico joins in too, barking his head off, and all around the playground you can hear similar gasps and shouts and cheers of joy as parents read the letter.

Lucinda's mum comes running over to us, beaming from ear to ear.

'We did it!' she says, throwing her arms around Mum.

'Yes,' says Mum, hugging her back. 'We certainly did!' Behind Lucinda's mum's back she and Dad grin at each other.

'Who do you think it is?' asks Lucinda's mum. 'This mysterious benefactor?'

'No idea!' says Dad. 'Come on kids. Let's go home and tell the others the good news.'

I skip home holding my dad's hand, happy as sunshine. Behind me I can hear V and Stanley chattering away excitedly, telling Mum all about our special assembly when Mrs Dunnet broke the good news. She wants to hear every little detail.

'That was kind of the Anonymous Benefactor, wasn't it, Dad?' I say.

'Very kind,' he agrees.

'I can't wait to tell Dontie. And Grandma and Granddad and Uncle Vez. They're going to be pleased, aren't they, Dad?'

'Very pleased, Mattie,' he says and gives my hand a squeeze. I'm glad that my dad's here with my mum to walk home with us on this special day. 'Tell you what,' he says. 'First one home gets to tell them.'

'Race you!' I shout and shoot off straight away, with the others chasing after me; V shrieking, 'That's not fair!' Stanley, knees up, elbows out, Dad with Anika wobbling about on his shoulders, Mum with the buggy, Will bouncing up and down inside it, and Jellico with his leg caught up in the lead.

My funny family races home to spread the news that we've saved our school.

And guess who wins?

ME!

Praise for My Funny Family

19th July 2013

Dear Chris Higgins.
        Your Funny Family books are really good. You are
better than JK Rowling, Roald Dahl and Enid Blyton! My mummy
and me are reading My Funny family books for the second time
and my favourite characters are Stanika. We love them so much
that we think you should write some more!
        Lots of love from Owen Parr xxx
                (Age eight)

Questions for the Author

1. What gave you the idea for the My Funny Family series?

Like most people my age I was brought up reading Enid Blyton. I loved her books but the world they were set in was so different from mine. The characters were so posh!

Then I discovered a wonderful writer called Eve Garnett who had written a book called *The Family from One-End Street* and this family was just like mine.

I haven't read them since I was nine but I think it was probably their influence that led me to write a series many, many years later about the adventures of a funny, loving, slightly chaotic family called the Butterfields.

2. Are any of the characters based on people in your funny family?

Stanika is based on my two eldest children, Kate and Pippa. Kate is two and a bit years older than Pippa but Kate was very small for her age and Pippa was very big. Pippa always used to sit on her big sister's lap and then Kate would disappear and all you could see was Pippa with Kate's hands and feet peeping out from behind her, just like Stanika.

We don't call them Kippa though.

3. Who is your favourite Butterfield?

That's like asking me who's my favourite child!

OK. If I have to make a choice I'd say Mattie is the most interesting with her worries and her observations. Though I have a soft spot for V who's a cross-patch but fiercely loyal. And then there's serious, dependable little Stanley ... and cute little Anika ... and I'm very fond of Grandma ...

See what I mean? It's impossible! But I'd love to know who you like best!

4. What's next for the Butterfields?

You'll be pleased to know that 'My Funny Family Gets Funnier.' That's actually the title of my next book! And after that the Butterfields go on a fabulous adventure, the most exciting yet, in a book called *My Funny Family Down Under*. Look out for them both soon!

5. What advice would you give to young writers?

There is lots of advice on my website www.chrishigginsthatsme.com

But the very best thing you can do if you want to become a writer is:

READ, READ, READ and WRITE, WRITE, WRITE!

6. When you were little, what did you want to be when you grew up?

At about the age of six or seven, one afternoon we all had to go out the front of the class one by one and tell everyone what we wanted to be when we left school.

I said I wanted to be an actress or an artist or a writer or a cowboy.

My teacher said, 'You can't be a cowboy, Christine, because you're a girl. You'll have to be a cowgirl,' and I was so disappointed. Cowgirls didn't seem to have as much fun as cowboys. So I said I'd be a writer instead.

Do go onto my website www.chrishigginsthatsme.com to find out more or get in touch.

Mattie is nine years old and she worries about everything, which isn't surprising. Because when you have a family as big and crazy as hers, there's always something to worry about! Will the seeds she's planted in the garden with her brothers and sisters grow into fruit and veg like everyone promised? Why does it seem as if Grandma doesn't like them sometimes? And what's wrong with Mum?

Read the first book in the hilarious and heart-warming young series about the chaotic life of the Butterfield family.

www.chrishigginsthatsme.com

Hodder
Children's
Books

my Funny Family

It's the summer holiday
and the Butterfield family
is going away to Cornwall.
As usual, Mattie has
plenty to worry about.
What if she loses the
luggage she's been put in
charge of? What if someone
falls over a cliff? And
worst of all ... what if
they've forgotten someone?

Read the second book in the hilarious and
heart-warming *My Funny Family* series.

Also available
as an ebook

www.chrishigginsthatsme.com

Hodder
Children's
Books

my **Funny** Family

It's the new school
term and, as the baby
inside Mum's tummy gets
bigger and bigger, the
family begins to plan
for Christmas. There
are lists to be made and
presents to be wrapped.
But could an unexpected
Christmas gift be just
around the corner?

Read the third book in the hilarious and
heart-warming *My Funny Family* series.

Collect all the
My Funny Family
books and discover more
of Mattie's adventures

Before writing her first novel, Chris Higgins taught English and Drama for many years in secondary schools and also worked at the Minack, the open-air theatre on the cliffs near Lands End. She now writes full time and is the author of eighteen books for children and teenagers.

Chris is married with four daughters. She loves to travel and has lived and worked in Australia as well as hitchhiking to Istanbul and across the Serengeti Plain. Born and brought up in South Wales, she now lives in the far west of Cornwall with her husband.